There Are All Kinds Of Bullies
So What's A Kid To Do?

Written By Julie Hernandez, BA
NY State Retired CASAC, Certified Life Coach
Illustrated By Eileen Sleckman

Briley & Baxter Publications | Plymouth, Massachusetts

ISBN: 978-1-954819-01-6

Book Design: Stacy O'Halloran

Some bullies look like giants. When they walk up to you, they look ten feet tall. They may use their strength to hurt you or use physical intimidation to scare you.

There is power and safety in numbers. Avoid going places by yourself.

If a bully is threatening you, make sure to stay with your friends. Make a pact that if anyone tries to pick on one of you, the others will go get help.

Do not try to fight with a bully. Know when you are in a dangerous situation and walk away. A bully looks for trouble. A hero avoids trouble and looks for peaceful solutions. Be a hero.

Before you say something, make sure that the words that come out of your mouth are not going to hurt someone else's feelings. Kids who say mean things to other people probably have someone in their lives saying mean things to them.

Try being nice to a bully. They will find it harder to pick on you.

You may feel tempted to say something mean to someone who is bullying you, but the bully is much better than you at being rude. Do you really want to be like the bully? No. Be kind instead.

Some bullies pretend to be your friends, but they are really your enemies.

True friends respect each other and do not talk behind each other's back.

If your "friends" are mean to you, do not try to make them like you. Act as if their words do not bother you.

Spend time with friends who you trust—those who make you feel good about yourself.

Some bullies use words to put you down.

Words can hurt very much, but they are only words.

It is what you think about yourself that is important.

Keep all the people who love you in mind.

It is their words that matter most.

Some kids may bully you through text messages or social media. There are steps you can take to prevent this.

Make sure to block anyone who tries to harass you through your computer or phone.

Tell a teacher, a parent, or an adult you trust what happened.

Stop communication with the bully immediately.

Do not allow strangers or bullies to be your friends online.

Make a pact with your friends that they will not respond to anything a bully says.

Bullies are not always other kids; sometimes they are adults.

An adult is a bully if he or she calls you names, laughs at you, insults you, or tries to physically harm you or touch you in any way that causes pain or makes you feel uncomfortable.

Always tell someone you trust if an adult harms you physically or verbally.

No one has the right to curse at you, yell at you, touch you, or hit you for any reason.

Never keep it a secret. Even if a bully threatens you, speak up!

Bullies can be members of your own family. In fact, some of the most difficult bullies to deal with are those who live with you—like an older brother or sister.

It is important to tell another family member that you are being bullied. There are also things you can say to protect yourself.

Be assertive. This means admitting, "I feel sad" or "I feel hurt when you say mean things to me."

You must also try your best to be kind when someone is being mean. Bullies are likely looking for a fight; do not give them what they want.

If a kid comes up to you and says something mean about what you are wearing, look him or her in the eye and say, "That's only your opinion. I like my shirt, skirt, or hat. It's okay if you don't like what I have on. I like your outfit, though." This will disarm the bully. You can also say, "Why does what I wear matter to you?"

If someone says, "I don't like you," you can say, "That's how you feel, but I like myself," or say "My friends like me, so it's okay if you don't."

Say something positive and then walk away. Another thing you can do is say something funny. Humor is a great way to change someone else's mood.

Don't let a bully take what is yours. Defend yourself and your property.

There will always be bullies in the world. It is your choice to let them make you feel bad about yourself.

Ignore their opinions. If a bully does not like you, who cares?

Do not let what they say affect how you feel about yourself. In most cases, they do not even know you.

Some bullies live inside of you.

Do you sometimes act like a bully? Are you sometimes mean to other kids or to your brothers and sisters?

How do you feel when you make someone else feel bad? Do you feel more powerful?

Do you feel bad when you hurt others?

It is good to feel bad for other people when they are sad or hurt. This is called empathy, and it keeps people from becoming bullies.

When you are face-to-face with a bully, keep these things in mind:

Be assertive. Assertive means showing respect and getting respect from others while standing up for yourself.

Walk tall with your head up. Looking down makes you seem insecure or afraid.

When you see someone being bullied, do not just watch or laugh.

Attitude matters. If you are nice to others, chances are they will be nice to you. If you treat others with respect, hopefully they will also respect you. If you are mean to others, they will either get angry or not like you. No one wants to be around a bully.

We are all unique in different ways, whether it is our skin color, nationalities, family traditions, religion, size, shape, or personality. Everyone is different. Honor those differences. Do not make fun of them. Imagine if everyone was the same? The world would be a boring place!

You can make a difference. So, why not start today? Practice being kind, and always look for the best traits in your friends. Be loyal and honest. Have fun engaging in activities you and your friends enjoy.

Do not allow jealousy or envy to enter your relationships. Instead, be happy when other people succeed, and don't forget to identify things that are special about you.

Write down some of your thoughts and feelings about bullies.

What are some ways you can avoid getting involved with a bully?

Make a list of things you can do if you end up in a bad situation with a bully. This way you will be prepared.

How do you feel about yourself?

How do others treat you?

Words That Describe A Bully:

Aggressive
Mean
Boastful
Rude
Critical
Bossy
Cruel
Attacking
Selfish
Jealous
Untrustworthy
Unhappy
Temper
Angry
Insulting

Words that Describe A Kind Person:

Polite
Loyal
Nice
Friendly
Happy
Fair
Assertive
Confident
Helpful
Supportive
Considerate
Thoughtful
Loving
Looks for Best in Others
Good

About the Author

Julie Hernandez has been in the field of addiction, co-dependency, trauma, grief, parenting, and anti-bullying work for over forty years. She was a co-founder of one of the largest counseling centers on Long Island and worked as director of community relations on Long Island for a group of psychiatric hospitals and substance abuse facilities. She also hosted "Spotlight on the Issues" a radio show on WLIE. Julie has been on numerous non-profit boards, including president of New Perspectives: an organization whose mission focused on anti-bullying. She appeared on MSNBC and CNN to help families of plane crash victims, as she lost her own father in a commercial airline crash as a child. She has been quoted in Time magazine and the New York Post, and she has appeared on TV and in a few documentaries about her work in the aftermath of the World Trade Center attacks. She has numerous honors for her volunteer work, including being in the circle of heroes at the Barnum and Bailey Circus. Newsday and Women's World have both featured her life story. She lives in Northport, New York with her husband of forty-three years, Rich. They have two married children and five grandchildren.

CPSIA information can be obtained
at www.ICGtesting.com
Printed in the USA
LVHW072338120421
684330LV00006B/54